Emily

Based on
The Railway Series
by the
Rev. W. Awdry

Illustrations by
**Robin Davies and
Jerry Smith**

EGMONT

EGMONT

We bring stories to life

First published in Great Britain in 2016
by Egmont UK Limited
The Yellow Building, 1 Nicholas Road, London W11 4AN

Thomas the Tank Engine & Friends™

CREATED BY BRITT ALLCROFT

HiT entertainment

ISBN 978 1 4052 7980 2
62421/1
Printed in Italy

Written by Emily Stead. Designed by Claire Yeo.
Series designed by Martin Aggett.

FSC
MIX
Paper
FSC® C018306

This story is about Emily,
who came to join the Steam Team
on Sodor. At first, some of the
engines weren't very friendly
to her – Emily wondered what
she had done wrong . . .

It was Emily's first day on The Fat Controller's Railway. She was a beautiful engine, with dark green paint and shiny brass fittings.

"Meet Emily," The Fat Controller said to Thomas.

"Peep! Peep!" whistled Thomas, and Emily smiled.

"Are you ready to collect your coaches, Emily?" asked The Fat Controller.

"Yes, Sir!" said Emily.

Emily steamed away, but the only coaches she could find were Annie and Clarabel. Emily's Driver coupled them up behind her.

Annie and Clarabel were not happy. "Thomas won't like this," grumbled Clarabel.

Emily passed Edward and Percy further down the track. She **whistled** a friendly hello, but the engines both pulled angry faces.

Just then, Thomas came puffing down the line.

"Peep! Peep! Hello, Thomas!" Emily called.

But when Thomas saw that Emily was pulling **his** coaches, he looked cross too!

Emily chuffed away, feeling sad. She didn't know why all the engines were being so rude to her.

The Fat Controller came to meet Thomas at Maithwaite Station.

"I want you to collect some new coaches from the Docks," he told Thomas. "Off you go."

"New coaches?" thought Thomas.

Thomas' wheels **wobbled** with worry. He thought the new coaches were for him. He didn't want new coaches — he wanted to keep Annie and Clarabel!

Later that day, Oliver met Emily in the Yard.

"What are you doing with Thomas' coaches?" Oliver shouted.

Emily felt **terrible**. "No wonder Thomas was cross!" she thought. "I must take Annie and Clarabel back to him, right away."

Emily set off, but soon had to stop again. Oliver had broken down on the track crossing.

Suddenly, Emily heard a **clickety-clack** on the track ahead. It was Thomas, and he was steaming straight towards Oliver!

"Bust my buffers!" cried Emily. "Thomas will never stop in time."

She **biffed** Oliver, pushing him over the crossing, just before Thomas rocketed past!

Emily had saved Thomas and Oliver!

"What a brave engine you are, Emily!"
The Fat Controller said proudly. "So here is
a special surprise — your very own coaches."

"Thank you, Sir!" smiled Emily. "I'm sorry I took
Annie and Clarabel, Thomas."

"And I'm sorry for being cross," said Thomas.

Emily was happy. Now she had two new coaches
and a new best friend!

The next day, Emily's job was to take trucks of flour to the Bakery. But the naughty trucks made Emily late.

"If you are late again, you will do Black Loch Run instead of pulling the Flour Mill Special," The Fat Controller boomed.

Emily promised to be on time. She didn't want to do the scary Black Loch Run — she had heard that a **monster** lived in the loch!

But the next day, the trucks were naughty again. They made Emily set off too soon, and half the trucks were left behind.

The Bakery Manager was not happy when Emily only delivered half the flour! She raced back to collect the rest of the trucks.

BIFF! Emily shunted them hard, but the trucks had taken off their brakes and rolled into the duck pond. **SPLASH!** What a sticky mess!

The next morning, The Fat Controller came to see Emily. "You are to take over the Black Loch Run," he told her.

Thomas gasped and Emily frowned. What about the **Black Loch Monster**?

She puffed sadly to the station, where lots of excited passengers were waiting.

"I must be brave," said Emily. And soon she was steaming up hills and through valleys.

At last, Emily reached the Black Loch. Her boiler **bubbled** as a strange shape splashed in the water.

But it wasn't a **monster** – it was a family of friendly seals! Emily smiled a big smile.

The next day, Thomas came to watch the seals too. Both engines agreed that the Black Loch Run wasn't scary, after all.

"Things aren't always what they seem," said Thomas wisely.

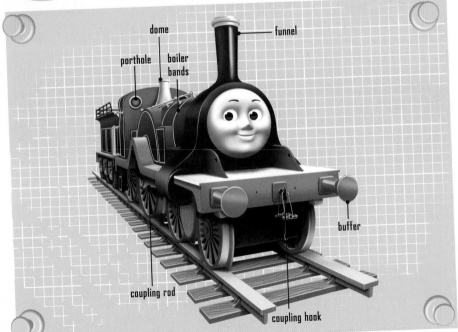

dome

funnel

porthole

boiler bands

buffer

coupling rod

coupling hook

Emily's challenge to you

Look back through the pages of this book
and see if you can spot:

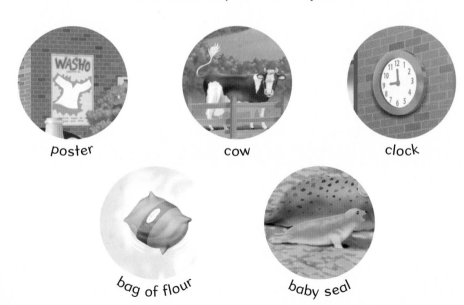

poster

cow

clock

bag of flour

baby seal

THE **THOMAS** ENGINE ADVENTURES

From Thomas to Harold the Helicopter, there is an Engine Adventure to thrill every Thomas fan.

 Thomas
 James
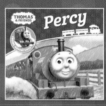 Percy
 Harold

 Spencer
 Henry
 Toby
 Gordon

 Cranky
 Flynn
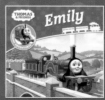 Emily
 Hiro